BABAR ™

BUMPER STORYBOOK

Adapted by Lesley Young
Illustrated by Clic Design

CHAD VALLEY

Based on the animated series "Babar"
a Nelvana-Ellipse Presentation,
a Nelvana Production in Association
with the Clifford Ross Company

Based on characters created by
Jean and Laurent de Brunhoff

Printed for Chad Valley Books
242-246 Marylebone Road, London NW1 6JL

ISBN 0 00 192 486 9

Printed by OFSAS.p.a.,(Casarile), Milan, Italy

BABAR™

BABAR'S
FIRST STEP

It was a special day in Celesteville - Babar was going to speak to his people. But, as captain of the football team, Alexander was supposed to be at a football match instead.

"I'm not playing," said Alexander, "Why should I? We're last!"

"Oh dear," sighed Babar, "let me explain about responsibility…"

Deep in the jungle all the creatures stopped to listen: "Baa-baar!" In a clearing a mother elephant cradled her new baby.

The other elephants had come to see him as his first trumpetings rose in the hot air: "Baa-baar!"

At last the old King said, "We must choose a name for him."

"Baa-baar!" bleated the new calf.

"Let's call him Babar," said his mother.

And all the elephants agreed that Babar was a very good name.

As Babar grew, he explored the jungle. His mother was always there to tell him about poisonous berries, or how to use his trunk.

But Babar was determined to learn some things for himself. One day he came across a dead tree stump blocking the path. The other elephants stepped over it, but Babar was too small. So he put his trunk round it and tugged and tugged. But only a small twig broke off, sending him reeling backwards.

Whenever Babar passed the tree stump he stopped and tried to move it, but it was always too heavy.

That day the elephants were gathering fruit from a tall tree. It was much too tall for the calves to reach. Babar tried to help. He charged forward and jumped, but only landed heavily on the ground: "Ouch!"

A monkey in the fruit tree above Babar started pointing at him and laughing.

Babar looked up, then he got to his feet and began doing a very silly dance right underneath.

"Do you think that fall affected Babar?" asked a worried Cornelius.

"Of course not," said Babar's mother. "He must have a plan."

Babar was twirling round now, looking funnier than ever. The monkey in the tree was laughing so hard that the branches shook.

Suddenly, fruit began raining down on the elephants. Babar stopped dancing and rushed with the others to scoop it up.

"Well, he certainly knows how to use his head," said Cornelius.

"And how to have fun," added his mother, proudly.

Suddenly a dreadful noise rang through the jungle.

BOOM!

Babar's mother rushed to his side. The noise came again - **BOOM!** The elephants ran off, mashing the fallen fruit to pulp under their feet.

Safe in the middle of some thick bushes the elephants gathered to discuss what to do.

"We don't know what the noise is, and we won't wait to find out," said the King. "Elephants - get in line. We're moving on."

Babar stepped forward. "But we want to stay here!" he shouted. "This is our home!"

"He's right," said his mother. "We can't just give it up."

Everyone looked at the King. "All those who think we should stay, raise your trunks," he boomed.

Slowly all the elephants raised their trunks.

"That's that," said the King. "We stay."

The elephants went off to play by the river, but nobody noticed a shadowy figure watching them.

Babar flung himself into the river. He swam underwater using his trunk like a snorkel. But when Babar surfaced he was met by Arthur, who shot a trunkful of water into his face.

Arthur ran off. Babar followed him and hosed him down with his trunk, only to find that he had hosed Celeste! "Hey!" she yelled.

"I didn't know it was you!" cried Babar. Arthur popped up beside Celeste. He drenched Babar again, then hid behind Celeste.

"This is what you do when you're not advising the King!" she said.

Babar blushed. "Oh - you heard."

"What do you think the terrible sound was?" Celeste asked.

Arthur pushed his way between them. "That's easy! It was a monster!"

"Once we know what it is, we'll be able to deal with it." said Babar. "Don't worry, Celeste."

Suddenly, he and Celeste were both drenched in water again.

They began to chase Arthur and had almost caught him when they heard the noise again: **BOOM!**

"Look after the children," cried Babar's mother to Cornelius. **BOOM!**

Cornelius herded the children together with his trunk. From the corner of his eye Babar could see his mother breaking away from the herd. She charged at the evil hunter and his gun!

The hunter aimed at Babar's mother. **BOOM!**

Although she was hit, Babar's mother kept charging. The hunter turned to run away. Before he went, he shot once more - **BOOM!**

Babar's mother sank down on to the soft jungle floor.

Later, Babar started to look for his mother. "Babar!" called Celeste, from behind some bushes. "I've been looking everywhere for you."

Then Cornelius slowly plodded towards them.

"Cornelius," said Babar, "have you seen my mother?"

Cornelius put his trunk gently round Babar. "Yes Babar," he said.

Cornelius took him to the edge of a small clearing. The elephant herd was standing in a circle. In the middle lay Babar's mother.

The tears rolled down Babar's tusks as he raised his small trunk and trumpeted.

"I'm sorry Babar - she's dead," said Cornelius.

Cornelius held Babar as he wept, and the other elephants swayed from side to side in a sad dance.

"...So that is why you never knew your dear grandmother," said Babar to his children.

A tear ran down Alexander's cheek. "That was so sad, Father."

"I have never forgotten my brave mother," sighed Babar. "But good can come out of bad. The elephants were about to start on a new life."

"And the hunter - did he come back?" asked Alexander.

"He did!" said Babar. "And this is what happened..."

After Babar had said goodbye to his mother he walked off alone until he came to the old tree stump.

He remembered how his mother had laughed when he had tried to lift it. Babar wrapped his trunk round the stump and pulled with all his strength, but it wouldn't budge.

"It's no use," thought Babar sadly.

Then Babar remembered how his mother had always tried to cheer him up when he tried hard - "Come on, little Babar!"

Babar stood up and gathered all his strength for one last try. He gripped the stump, dug his feet into the ground, and pulled.

Just as he was about to give up, one tiny root popped free, then more, until at last the whole mass of twisted roots came up, freeing the stump. Babar lay back on the ground, panting.

Pushing the stump aside, Babar slowly got to his feet and took one wobbly step forward. Using all his remaining strength, he trumpeted. Now he could go on.

Cornelius had been watching from behind a bush.

"Yes - Babar is destined for great things," he said to himself.

Days later, Celeste was looking for her brother. "Arthur, where are you?" she called.

"Looking for this?" grinned Babar, emerging from a bush and pushing Arthur into view with his trunk.

"I'm not afraid of the hunter!" said Arthur, tripping over backwards.

"Come on, Arthur," smiled Babar, "let's play follow my leader."

"All right, I'll be the leader," began Arthur. But Babar and Celeste had already started, and he had to hurry behind.

All three of them were out of breath when they arrived back in the clearing. They didn't know that the hunter had returned and was watching them.

Pompadour was speaking to the King, "There is a place I have heard of that is so deep in the jungle, that even the hunter would never find us. We should go there."

Babar stepped forward and said, "But this is our home. We must stay here."

"We all feel the way you do," said the King, "but it's a question of survival."

Pompadour was growing more nervous. "We're no match for the hunter," he said. "We must leave NOW, before it's too late!"

But before they could move, there was an ear-splitting **BOOM!** and a branch crashed down on the King.

The elephants saw the evil hunter stride out of the bushes and raise his rifle. They ran off in a panic, with Arthur, Cornelius and Pompadour helping the King.

"Run, Babar! Run!" shouted Celeste. Babar raced after the others. Then suddenly he veered round and began to head back in the other direction. They all watched in horror as Babar charged towards the hunter, who was reloading his gun.

Babar trumpeted and drew the hunter's attention away from the rest of the herd.

BOOM! The hunter fired, but now Babar was charging off in another direction. The hunter followed.

"Must keep him away from the others," panted Babar. **BOOM!** The hunter fired again. Babar hurled himself at the hunter, who fell over.

Then he ran off through a tunnel of creepers. But there was the hunter, raising his gun! Babar turned and raced back again. He could hear the hunter behind him.

The hunter had Babar in his sights. It was a clear shot, with nothing in between. He closed his finger over the trigger...

But then Babar recognised where he was - this was where he had pulled up the stubborn tree stump! He saw the crater looming up in front of him and took a flying leap, landing safely on the other side.

But the hunter didn't know about the hole. He was aiming his rifle and he didn't see the crater opening up in front of his feet until he had fallen right into it.

As he fell, the hunter's gun went flying. Babar grabbed it with his trunk and threw it far into the jungle. Then, leaving the hunter in the hole, he turned and ran away.

He did not stop running for days - not until he came to a lonely ledge, far away from the friends he loved and had saved. He knew that they were now safe in the heart of the jungle.

Babar knew that there was more to be done. He knew that he must help them find a way of living peacefully, safe from the hunter and his gun.

Babar sat down and stared before him. In the distance he could see the bright lights of the city. They seemed to call him…

"So you saved the whole elephant tribe?" said Alexander. "But what did you do next?"

"That's another story," laughed Babar. "But I made some wonderful friends."

He looked over at the Old Lady, and smiled. "And you discovered that not everyone in the city is like the hunter," she said, quietly.

"I don't understand what all this has got to do with responsibility," said Alexander.

"Responsibility means that you can't always do what you want to do," said Babar. "We can tell what people, or kings, are like by the way they handle responsibilities to others."

"Like your mother putting the rest of the tribe before herself?" asked Alexander.

"Exactly," said Babar. "I think you've understood the story after all."

Then Babar turned towards the balcony doors. Through them he could hear the people of Celesteville cheering.

"Are you coming on to the balcony, Alexander?" he asked.

Alexander hesitated only a moment. "If you don't mind," he said, "I think I'll join my football team. I think it's my responsibility - after all, I'm the captain."

"I don't mind at all," said Babar. "I think it's a very good idea."

As Alexander went off, Celeste smiled at Babar, "You're a very special father."

"And that," said the Old Lady as they stepped out on to the balcony, "is what makes him such a special King!"

BABAR
RETURNS

It was night in Celesteville and the whole palace was in darkness, except for the kitchen. Light was streaming from the open fridge as Flora rummaged through the shelves. "Mangoes, tangerines, bananas, marzipan on toast…"

"That's the kind of midnight snack that will give you nightmares," said a deep voice behind her. "Why are you up so late?"

"It's the tennis match tomorrow," said Flora. "I'm so worried about it I can't sleep. You see, I'm always missing shots and Alexander gets furious with me."

"Perhaps you should stop thinking about your weaknesses and find out if your opponents have any," said Babar.

Flora looked puzzled. "Can you explain?"

Babar put a pile of food on the table and settled down. As he spread butter on the bread, Babar began, "A long time ago…"

It was a busy day in the city and Babar was watching the people from the balcony of the Old Lady's house. Although the sun was shining, and all the birds were singing, Babar looked sad and his trunk drooped.

The Old Lady joined him on the balcony. "Good morning, Babar. What a lovely day!"

"I suppose it is," sighed Babar.

"Does the sunshine make you sad?" asked the Old Lady, kindly.

"I was just thinking about…" Babar began, looking at the trees.

The Old Lady understood. "I know - Celeste, Arthur and Cornelius. Cheer up - let's go for a walk."

Babar was looking through his binoculars as he and the Old Lady walked along. Suddenly, he put them down and rubbed his eyes.

"What is it, Babar?" asked the Old Lady.

"Nothing," said Babar. " I'm imagining things."

But then he heard, "Babar! Babar!" There were Celeste and Arthur looking at him from behind the bushes. He stood up as they ran towards him, crying.

"Is it really you? How did you get here?" asked Babar.

"When you didn't return we came to look for you," said Celeste.

"But we got lost!" said Arthur. "I knew we'd find you if we got lost enough… I'm hungry," he added.

"Then I know just the place to take you," said the Old Lady. She took them to a cake shop that sold plump cream puffs.

"There's nothing like this in the jungle," said Arthur, happily.

"Now we must do some shopping," said the Old Lady. She took them to a clothes shop where Arthur found a smart sailor suit and Celeste chose a white dress.

In a perfume shop the Old Lady chose some dusting powder and a scent spray for Celeste.

"Now for music!" cried the Old Lady, leading the way into a music shop where she bought them a fine gramophone and some records.

"We mustn't forget fun!" said the Old Lady, and off they went to a toy shop where they were all kitted out with roller skates.

"Thank you!" they all cried.

Back in her parlour the Old Lady poured tea. "We came to bring you back home, Babar," said Celeste. "We all need you."

Arthur helped himself to another cream puff. "It's terrible. The hunter is chasing us deeper and deeper into the jungle."

The hunter! Babar turned icy cold at the words. It was the hunter who had shot his mother, leaving Babar to fend for himself.

"You must go - they need your help," said the Old Lady.

"I know," agreed Babar. Together they packed up all their presents into the little red car. "I am going to miss you," said the Old Lady.

"Thank you for everything," said Babar. Then the car sped off, with the Old Lady waving and Babar calling, "I'll come back one day!"

Soon they were travelling over mountains and across bridges until Babar could see the jungle in the distance, throbbing under a cloud of heat. "It's good to be back," he said.

"We're not there yet," said Celeste. "We go down there." She pointed down a damp track to a dark and gloomy clearing.

"But that's the darkest, most miserable part of the whole jungle," said Babar.

As they stared unhappily into the dark, they heard a noise...

The bushes round about them
were shaking as if they were alive.
Celeste and Arthur huddled close to
Babar as he pulled out his walking
stick and lashed at the bushes.

"Hey! Careful there!" Three pairs
of tusks emerged, joined to
Pompadour, Cornelius, and Celeste
and Arthur's mother who hurried to
hug her children.

"How are you, Pompadour?" asked
Babar.

"Lucky to be alive, all things
considered," rumbled the elephant.
"But what's happened to you?
You're as green as creepers!"

"This is just a suit," said Babar.
"It can come off, you know." He
took off his jacket.

"My tusks!" boomed Cornelius.
"You can shed your skin - just like a
snake!"

"I'm glad I've found you all safe and sound," said Babar.

"You're lucky you found us at all," said Pompadour.

"We kept moving," explained Cornelius, "thinking we would find a really safe place, but now we realise there is no such thing."

"No - not even this miserable place," said the old King, who was coming out of the bushes. He looked older than ever.

Suddenly there was a roar, and the sound of something heavy crashing through the undergrowth. "It's the hunter!" cried Pompadour. "Run!"

The elephants tore off in all directions. "Hurry, run, Babar!" trumpeted Cornelius.

Babar jumped into his car and tried desperately to start the engine. Nothing happened. Behind him he could hear the hunter's jeep coming nearer. Suddenly the car leapt forward and Babar drove off as fast as he could into the jungle.

That night the elephants gathered to make plans. The King stood on a mound of earth and boomed, "We will run no further. Tomorrow we will drive the hunter away. I call for an elephant stampede!"

Babar stepped forward and said, "Your Highness, this is madness. The hunter has a gun - we must beat him by using our wits."

"You have been away too long," said Cornelius, softly. "You have forgotten what jungle-life is like."

"Has Babar forgotten, too, that the stampede is a great elephant tradition?" said the King. "I have spoken. It will be done!"

Next morning Babar and Celeste watched the sunrise. "Tell me again about the opera," said Celeste.

"I think that's what put Arthur to sleep at last!" said Babar.

"If the hunter catches us, we'll see it all from inside…" Celeste began.

"Cages," shuddered Babar. "Not if I can help it."

At the same time, all the other elephants were forming a long line. They were led by the King, and each animal gripped the tail of the one in front.

One elephant just watched the procession. He was too old to join the stampede. Then the line disappeared into the distance with the elephants' war chant fading as it went.

Suddenly Babar, Celeste and Arthur burst into the clearing. Babar was in a panic. "Quick - where are the others?" he asked the old elephant, breathlessly.

"They've left for the stampede, of course," he answered.

"Come on," said Babar to Celeste and Arthur. "They can't have gone far. We can catch up with them."

"You won't be able to stop them," the old elephant called after them.

But Babar and the others were too late. At the hunter's camp, all the elephants were locked inside a corral he had built from logs. The hunter walked around it, slapping his leg with his riding crop and laughing loudly with an evil laugh.

The King turned to Cornelius, "What is this ivory he speaks of?"

"I believe, Your Majesty, he is talking about our tusks," replied Cornelius. "I've heard they are worth quite a fortune when they sell them in the big cities."

"How horrible," shuddered the King, sending ripples down his folds of grey skin. "I have failed my people. I should have listened to Babar - he knew that the hunter would trick us into this trap."

The elephants stared sadly out of the corral, not knowing what was going to happen next.

Babar parted the bushes and looked across to the corral. "We're too late," he groaned. "The hunter has trapped everyone."

"It's all over," moaned Celeste.

"No it's not," said Babar. He stretched out his trunk and whispered to the others.

A few minutes later the hunter heard war-like music echoing through the jungle. He grabbed his gun and rushed off to see where it was coming from.

Babar watched him hurry past. "Now!" he whispered to the others. They rushed to the corral and heaved at the gate. The trapped elephants pushed from inside.

At last the gate gave way and the elephants poured out. "Go to the river!" cried Babar.

Then the hunter found the hidden gramophone that the Old Lady had bought Babar, and realised he'd been tricked…

The hunter came back into the clearing just in time to see the last of the elephants streaming into the jungle. He raised his rifle and prepared to fire.

At that moment Babar appeared, holding Celeste's perfume spray. He squirted it right into the evil hunter's eyes. The hunter cried and staggered backwards.

Babar raced through the jungle after the others. At the river's edge he turned and waited for the hunter, standing at the edge of a wide log. The hunter climbed on to the log and aimed his rifle at Babar. Babar yelled, "Now, Arthur!"

Arthur pulled a vine attached to a piece of wood wedged in front of the log. As it came out, it freed the roller skates that Babar had tied to the log. The log zoomed down the bank carrying the hunter towards the river where crocodiles were swimming hungrily.

"Hooray!" shouted the elephants. But their joy was short-lived. Next morning they found the old king lying beside a patch of strange-looking mushrooms. His skin looked odd and shrivelled.

"What is it?" asked Babar, as one of the mushrooms fell out of the King's mouth.

"These mushrooms must be poisonous," said Cornelius, as the King rolled over. A hush fell over the jungle. The king was dead.

"This is a dreadful place," cried Babar. "We must leave here and never return."

So the elephants formed a sad line and walked until they reached their old home.

The grass was bright, and the air was clean and fresh. The elephants trumpeted happily. Some splashed in the river, while others shook fruit off the trees.

"It's so good to be home," sighed Celeste.

Pompadour called for attention. "It is now our duty to appoint a new king. There is only one among us who has the wisdom and the vision to lead us."

Cornelius stepped forward. "Well, thank you for the compliment," he said, "but I'm afraid I cannot accept. Babar is the one who must be king."

Pompadour snorted crossly - he had been about to choose Babar himself!

"Long live King Babar!" trumpeted the whole herd of elephants.

Babar knelt as Cornelius placed the crown on his head. Then he stood up and called for silence.

"The days of running and hiding, and living in fear are over. The jungle is changing all around us, and we must learn to change with it. I promise that together we will grow strong and happy."

The elephants trumpeted a happy salute.

"And that," said Babar to Flora, "is how we defeated the evil hunter. We were able to do it because we knew his weaknesses. Of course," he added, "we were lucky too!"

"We thought we heard voices!" Celeste, Alexander and Pom appeared round the door.

"It's a good thing I made this a family-size sandwich," said Babar.

Flora turned to Alexander. "Have you ever noticed that Pom has a weak backhand?"

"As a matter of fact I have," said Alexander, grinning.

"I'm so excited I can't sleep," cried Flora. "I think we might win the tennis match!"

At last the three children went back to bed. "Suddenly I'm hungry," said Celeste. "Could I have one of your special sandwiches?"

"Of course," smiled Babar, "if you've got time. I can't leave out the most important ingredient - a good story!"

A PET FOR
BABAR

One morning Flora was very sad. One of her pet goldfish had died.

"Did you ever have a goldfish that died?" she asked, looking sadly at her remaining pet.

"No," said Babar, "but once I had to give up a pet I really loved. It all started when Rataxes, the Rhino King, tried to stir up trouble in Celesteville..."

In the palace, Cornelius was crossly pacing up and down. "This is dreadful," said Pompadour, "it's very disturbing."

"Disturbing?" roared Cornelius. "Why, it's diabolical, it's..." He spluttered down his trunk looking for the word.

"It's a blockade," said Pompadour.

"What's a blockade?" asked Babar.

"A blockade is the blocking of certain goods to prevent them getting to those who need them," said Pompadour.

"In this case, us," added Cornelius.

"But what is Rataxes keeping from us?" asked Babar. "Fuel? Medical supplies?"

"Much worse," said Cornelius. "Pomegranates!"

"Pomegranates?" said Babar in disbelief.

Cornelius picked one up from a bowl on Babar's desk. "This is the last pomegranate in the kingdom!"

"But why are pomegranates so important?" asked Babar at last.

Pompadour strutted over, took the pomegranate from Cornelius and dropped it in disgust. "Although I detest the fruit it plays a vital part in the livelihood of your subjects. No pomegranates means no pomegranate juice makers, and that means a loss of vitamin C and Riboflavin."

"My tusks!" cried Babar. "I can't let Rataxes get away with this!"

In the Rhino Palace, Rataxes was at his desk surrounded by piles of pomegranates.

"But what's so important about pomegranates?" Basil was asking.

"Nothing, Basil," said Rataxes. "It's the blockade that matters. Pomegranates are just the start of my plan to control Celesteville!"

Just then the door burst open and Muffy, the pet warthog, bounded in, followed by Lady Rataxes. Rataxes took a flying leap out of the way.

"You're getting him all excited," said Lady Rataxes. "He wants his walkies."

Muffy snapped and growled below Rataxes. "Why can't Basil take him?" he asked, then **"OUCH!"** as Muffy's teeth took a chunk out of the seat of his trousers.

"That was my last uniform!" he cried, falling into the pomegranates. Muffy dashed out of the way.

"You nearly squashed my baby!" said Lady Rataxes, angrily.

"Here," she commanded, "take Muffy for his walk. She gave his lead to Rataxes. The warthog ran outside, dragging a desperate Rataxes along behind him.

"He wants to be friends with you," called Lady Rataxes, as the warthog snarled and bared his teeth.

"Basil, don't leave me…" shouted Rataxes as he was pulled through the pomegranates.

In Babar's office, Cornelius was pacing up and down. "Please think again, Your Majesty. I'm sure we could bargain with Rataxes. We could exchange something."

"But Cornelius," said Babar, "they're *our* pomegranates. Why should we reward someone for stealing them from us?"

"We'll have to," said Cornelius.

Elephants could be heard outside. "Give us back our pomegranates!" "We want action!"

"I can't think here," said Babar. "I must find some peace and quiet."

Meanwhile, in the jungle, Rataxes was complaining. Behind him came Basil and Muffy. The warthog was trying to reach Rataxes.

"I've got a blockade to run," muttered Rataxes, and stopped in his tracks. "**OUCH!**" Muffy sank his teeth firmly into the seat of Rataxes' trousers.

"You didn't say you were going to stop!" said Basil.

Rataxes lifted Basil by the lapels. "That's the last bite of me he's going to get. Take Muffy for a walk, Basil. A long walk on a short path!"

Basil looked at him in horror. "You don't mean leave the poor little thing in the jungle, do you?" One look at Rataxes' face was enough.

Basil padded through the jungle with Muffy. He found a strong tree and tied the lead to it. "Sorry," he said, "but you heard him."

Then he heard someone coming. With a last wave, Basil dashed into the bushes.

In the jungle, Babar tripped over Muffy's lead and landed on the ground. Muffy leapt on top of him and began to lick him all over.

"Where did you come from?" asked Babar. "Oh - your lead has got tied to this tree." He untied Muffy. "You can go home now."

Muffy didn't budge. "You're lost!" said Babar. "I'll take you home and find you something to eat."

Basil watched them. "Wait till I tell Rataxes," he chuckled.

In Celesteville, the pomegranate panic was reaching new heights.

"We *must* make a deal with Rataxes," said Cornelius. "I've done the paperwork."

Just then Muffy dashed in, scattering the papers. "Perhaps you are too busy to have a new pet," suggested Cornelius.

Babar was patting Muffy. "We'll think of something, won't we boy?"

"He's taken the warthog as an adviser!" groaned Pompadour.

Back at the Rhino Palace, Lady Rataxes was *not* happy. "I'm sorry, my sweet," said Rataxes. "He broke his lead and ran off. I charged after him, risking life and limb, but there was no sign…"

Then he added, "You can have another pet. Something without teeth - I mean, teething troubles."

Lady Rataxes dropped limply on to a chair. She sobbed, "I want my Muffy. There is nothing I love so much, except you, and if you are still the man I married you'll bring him back to me!"

Rataxes backed out of the room, saying, "Of course, dear, of course!" He backed straight into Basil who had been listening.

"Muffy is in Celesteville," said Basil. "We shall have to steal him back."

"Let's go," growled Rataxes.

Babar and Muffy were playing in the palace gardens. They didn't notice that two bushes seemed to be following them.

"Fetch!" cried Babar, throwing a stick. Muffy followed it into the larger bush. "**OUCH!**"

Muffy reappeared with a patch of ripped cloth in his teeth, then licked Babar's face. "Are you hungry again?" said Babar. "Stay here - I'll fetch you some scraps."

Rataxes called, "I've come to take you home to mummy." Muffy snarled and leapt into the bush.

Babar was returning with the food when he saw Muffy chasing two bushes out of the garden. As he watched, the bushes jumped over the fence. There was a giant splash.

"Oh how I hate that hog!" cried Rataxes from the palace fountain.

"Rataxes!" called Babar. "What are you doing here?"

Babar held Muffy who growled and tried to reach Rataxes.

"I thought you'd be too busy with your blockade to pay a social call," said Babar to Rataxes, taking the two rhinos up to his office.

"What blockade?" asked Rataxes, innocently. Babar pointed at a solitary pomegranate.

"Oh - heh, heh - that blockade…"

"That blockade," said Babar. "And now I'm calling the guards."

"Wait!" said Basil. "The reason Lord Rataxes has come here is to talk about ending the blockade." Basil was playing for time. "We will lift the blockade in exchange for… for…well…"

"WHAT, Basil?" snapped Rataxes.

"Feathers!" cried Basil. "One thousand pounds of feathers!"

"No gold?" asked Rataxes. "And no land, or anything?"

"No - you're happy with feathers."

"Feathers…" repeated Rataxes in amazement.

Later, in the guest chamber, Rataxes asked Basil, "Why do I want all those feathers?"

"You don't want them, Your Righness," Basil replied.

Rataxes grabbed Basil by the lapels and pinned him on his horn. "Then tell me what I *do* want, Basil," he said coldly.

"You want to get Muffy back," said Basil, "and this is a trick."

Rataxes beamed and let Basil go. "I thought that's what I wanted!"

Meanwhile, Babar was looking for Muffy. "Time for your bath," he said. At the word 'bath', Muffy ran off. Babar went in search of him.

"Oh Muffy!" came a voice. Muffy turned to see a figure that looked like Lady Rataxes. As he watched, it walked towards him, tripped over the long dress and fell. "I've got you some beastie bites."

Muffy trotted up to the figure. To his horror, Rataxes' arm appeared and snapped on a lead. "Got you!"

"Miserable little hairball!" muttered Rataxes. "You won't get away again." For a moment Muffy was stunned, then he jumped out of Rataxes' arms and bolted, with Rataxes still holding on to the lead.

"BAAS-ILLL!!!" yelled Rataxes. "WHOAH BOY! WHOAH MUFFY!"

Basil chased after them. "Reel him in, Your Righness!"

In a nearby courtyard, Pompadour and Cornelius were gathering the feathers. A long line of naked jungle birds watched as Pompadour checked off his list. "Well, that's it - one thousand pounds exactly."

Cornelius stepped forward and spoke. "On behalf of His Majesty, I would like to thank you all for your help, your patriotism, and your..."

"Feathers?" suggested Pompadour.

The birds didn't get a chance to reply. There was a yelp and Muffy appeared. They watched in horror as he dragged Rataxes through the mound of feathers.

Muffy dragged Rataxes on to the courtyard and into the fountain with a giant splash. Cornelius, Pompadour and Babar arrived on the scene. "We do have an indoor bath," said Pompadour, smoothly.

Muffy leapt back into Babar's arms and licked his face. "We're so sorry about this," said Cornelius to Rataxes, "but I hope you noticed we *had* your feathers ready."

"Not so fast!" said Rataxes.

"If it's your dress that worries you," said Pompadour, "we'll have it cleaned…"

Basil was thinking fast. "Actually, I distinctly remember Lord Rataxes asked for *fuschia* feathers."

The elephants gazed at him in amazement. "Of course," agreed Rataxes. "Ordinary feathers are two a penny. What do you take me for - a fool?"

"That wasn't part of the deal and you know it," said Babar.

"Well, you can take it or leave it," said Rataxes, and he walked off.

"I'm trying to do what's best," said Babar, "but no one understands, except this little warthog."

"He's interfering with your duty as king," said Cornelius. "We should find another home for him."

"I'll never let him go," said Babar.

Outside the palace kitchen stood two suits of elephant armour. An echo rumbled out of the larger one. "As soon as we get that hog back home, I'm going to blockade EVERYTHING! Where is he?"

There was a clank, and Basil looked over to see Muffy attached to the armour's behind. "I think I've found him," he said.

Then Babar appeared. "Let go of my warthog!" he boomed.

Rataxes dashed through a nearby doorway. "But that's the stairs…" called Basil.

Pompadour and Cornelius were counting the last fuschia feathers. "That's it," said Pompadour. "One thousand pounds exactly."

Cornelius stepped forward. "On behalf of His Majesty," he said, "I would like to thank you for your help, patriotism, and your…"

"Fuschia feathers?" suggested Pompadour.

Suddenly Babar's voice rang out. "Guards! Stop that warthog!" Then Rataxes raced into view and landed in the feathers. Babar rushed up and grabbed Muffy.

"You want pomegranates?" roared Rataxes. "Give me that warthog!"

"But what about your feathers?" asked Pompadour.

"Keep them!" said Rataxes, spitting some out. "I want the hog!"

"Forget the pomegranates," said Babar, "I'm keeping him."

"Right," said Rataxes. "In that case…" But then he heard a familiar voice.

It was Lady Rataxes. "Oh Muffy!"

"Muffy?" said Babar, sadly. "It's your warthog?"

"King Babar, name your reward," smiled Lady Rataxes.

"Our pomegranates back," said Babar, promptly, "and an end to all blockades!"

"Done!" said Lady Rataxes.

"Do you know, I still miss that warthog," sighed Babar to Flora. "It's hard to say goodbye to something you love."

"But you were laughing while you told me about him," smiled Flora. "That's because we had a lot of fun together," Babar grinned. "Instead of wasting time missing old friends, we should always remember how good it was to know them."

Flora gave Babar a hug. "I'll remember."